GFFs

GHOST FRIENDS FOREVER

GFFs
GHOST FRIENDS FOREVER

#2 WITCHES GET THINGS DONE

STORY BY MONICA GALLAGHER
ART BY KATA KANE

charmZ
NEW YORK

GFFs
GHOST FRIENDS FOREVER

#2 "WITCHES GET THINGS DONE"

GFFs: GHOST FRIENDS FOREVER BY MONICA GALLAGHER & KATA KANE
©2018 MONICA GALLAGHER & KATA KANE
EDITORIAL ©2018 BY PAPERCUTZ
ALL RIGHTS RESERVED.

MONICA GALLAGHER – STORY
KATA KANE – ART & COVER
MATT HERMS – COLORS
WILSON RAMOS JR. – LETTERING

CHARMZ BOOKS MAY BE PURCHASED FOR BUSINESS OR PROMOTIONAL USE.
FOR INFORMATION ON BULK PURCHASES PLEASE CONTACT MACMILLAN
CORPORATE AND PREMIUM SALES DEPARTMENT AT (800) 221-7945 X5442

MARIAH McCOURT – ORIGINAL SERIES EDITOR
KATA KANE, JIM SALICRUP – EDITORS
JEFF WHITMAN – ASSISTANT MANAGING EDITOR
JIM SALICRUP
EDITOR-IN-CHIEF

PB ISBN: 978-1-5458-0151-2
HC ISBN: 978-1-5458-0150-5

PRINTED IN CHINA,
OCTOBER 2018

DISTRIBUTED BY MACMILLAN
FIRST PRINTING

LIKE, **MAGIC** TRAINING?

WE'LL TALK ABOUT IT IN THE MORNING. FOR NOW...

...TRY TO GET BACK TO SLEEP, OKAY? DO YOU NEED A GLASS OF WATER? BEDTIME STORY?

DAAAD.

SMEK

MAGIC TRAINING. IT'S **FINALLY** HAPPENING...

DING

Dear Whitney, I had the dream again last night.

Except this time the scary poltergeist had **TWO** heads and they looked like **US!** What does that mean?

I hope it means you're coming back soon! Why else would the dream show our faces together?

It's hard to walk by your bridge every day and not see you there.

It's hard to walk past Miss Fairweather's old classroom, where you **SAVED** all of us.

COOOOOL, A REAL-LIFE PSYCHIC? WE'VE HAD SOME FORTUNETELLERS HERE BEFORE, BUT THEY NEVER STICK AROUND LONG.

=AGH!= NOT TO SAY THAT **YOU AND YOUR MOM** WON'T BE HERE LONG!

NO WORRIES, WE PROBABLY WON'T BE... WE MOVE AROUND A LOT. THIS IS MY FOURTH NEW SCHOOL.

I JUST TRY NOT TO GET TOO COMFORTABLE WHERE I AM. AND I'M USED TO BEING BY MYSELF, SO IT'S NOT THAT BAD.

WELL, LIKE I SAID, I'M SOPHIA, AND I'M HAPPY TO SERVE AS YOUR FRIEND WHILE YOU'RE IN TOWN.

I'M CHARLOTTE.

FWUMP

TUESDAY EVENING.

SO ... WHAT EXACTLY ARE WE DOING HERE?

I'M BOOOORED...

PATIENCE, MIJA... YOUR MOTHER IS ALMOST DONE SETTING UP.

YEAH, BUT **WHAT'S** SHE SETTING UP? WHAT ARE WE HERE TO LEARN?

YOU'RE HERE TO LEARN THE BASICS OF GHOST IDENTIFICATION AND CATEGORIZATION.

REALLY? YOU'RE FINALLY LETTING US LEARN PARANORMAL STUFF?

IN A **CONTROLLED** ENVIRONMENT... YES.

SO WHAT DOES THAT... MEAN?

IT MEANS THAT YOU'RE GOING TO LEARN ALL ABOUT THE SCIENTIFIC METHODS AND EQUIPMENT WE USE IN THIS FAMILY TO ACCURATELY PREDICT, TRACK, AND ASSIST PARANORMAL BEINGS.

COOL!... SO WHEN DO WE GET TO LEARN MORE OF THE SPELL STUFF?

LIKE WHAT DAD CAN DO?

THEN LIKE WHAT FELIX DID WITH MISS FAIRWEATHER?

=GROAN!=

I NEVER WANT TO DO THAT STUFF AGAIN.

WHAT? WHY NOT?

DON'T WORRY, NEITHER OF YOU **WILL**...EVER AGAIN.

BECAUSE NIGHTMARES ARE JUST THE BEGINNING OF WHAT MESSING WITH SPELLS CAN DO.

...THAT IS **NOT** WHAT **YOU'RE** GOING TO BE LEARNING. NOT HERE, NOT NOW.

BUT--

AND BEFORE YOU COMPLAIN, WILL YOU PLEASE JUST TRY TO LISTEN TO WHAT I WANT TO TEACH YOU? I HAVE EXPERTISE, TOO.

BUT ALL WE **DO** IS YOUR WAY--?

...YES, MAMA.

WELL-BEHAVING CHILDREN IS MY CUE TO LEAVE!

CLAP

I'LL GET OUT OF YOUR MOTHER'S HAIR SO SHE CAN WORK.

SOPHIA, I'LL BE BACK IN TWO HOURS TO PICK YOU UP. TAKE CARE, MY LOVELIES!

OR...ER, I MEAN WE USED TO. MY PARENTS...AREN'T TOGETHER ANYMORE.

OH... SORRY.

IT'S FINE, IT'S NOT A BIG DEAL! I MEAN, IT'S BEEN OVER A YEAR NOW, I'M USED TO IT.

MY DAD'S BEEN OUT OF THE PICTURE SINCE I WAS A BABY.

BUT IT'S OKAY. I NEVER GOT TO KNOW HIM, SO I DON'T REALLY KNOW WHAT I'M MISSING.

SO WHAT'S NEXT ON THE TOUR?

UMMM...THAT'S PRETTY MUCH IT OTHER THAN THE PLACES IN TOWN KNOWN FOR THEIR PARTICULAR HAUNTINGS, BUT YOU PROBABLY DON'T WANT TO BE BORED BY ALL THAT!

I BET YOUR MOM WILL HEAR A LOT OF IT FROM TOWN LOCALS, TOO.

WHAT'S UP WITH THAT CREEPY COVERED BRIDGE IN THE WOODS? THAT'S GOT TO BE ONE OF THE HAUNTED SPOTS.

OH...IT IS, BUT...

WHOOPS, IS THAT A PLACE YOUR FAMILY USED TO GO, OR SOMETHING?

NO, THAT'S WHERE THIS GHOST GIRL WHITNEY, UM--THAT'S HER BRIDGE.

OH, SWEET! I'D LOVE TO MEET HER...I HAVEN'T REALLY GOTTEN TO MEET ANY OF THE TOWN'S FAMOUS GHOSTS YET.

I WISH YOU COULD, BUT SHE'S NOT THERE RIGHT NOW. SHE AND I...I MEAN...SHE'LL BE BACK SOON THOUGH!

I JUST KNOW SHE WILL BE.

HOW ABOUT FOR NOW WE GO CHECK OUT THE SCENE AT THE CRYPTID CAFE?

...AND WAIT TILL I TELL YOU WHAT HAPPENED **THERE!**

I'LL BE OUT OF HERE BEFORE YOU KNOW--

SNIFF *SNIFF*

HELLO?

DID THEY GET YOU, TOO?

DID...WHO GET ME?

HI, I'M UM, WHITNEY, WHAT'S YOUR NAME?

I . . . I DON'T REMEMBER.

ARE YOU OKAY?

UH-UH.

HEY, YOU'RE -- YOU'RE ALIVE! HOW DID YOU GET DOWN HERE IF YOU'RE ALIVE?

I . . . DON'T REMEMBER.

WELL, YOU'RE NOT ALONE ANYMORE.

AND I'M GOING TO GET US BOTH OUT OF HERE, DON'T YOU WORRY.

SPECTREVILLE HIGH SCHOOL.

HEY, SOPHIA, WHAT'S UP?

NOTHING, JAKE, WHY?

WELL...

I JUST HAVEN'T GOTTEN TO HANG OUT WITH YOU IN A WHILE. HOW ARE THINGS?

FINE.

⸮SIGH.⸮ SO-PHEEE...

STOP ACTING LIKE WE'RE STRANGERS. IF YOU'R STILL MAD AT ME AND YOU WANT TO IGNORE ME, JUST TELL ME! I'LL LEAVE YOU ALONE.

I'M NOT MAD AT YOU! WHY DO YOU THINK THAT?

BECAUSE YOU WON'T TALK TO ME... YOU BARELY **LOOK** AT ME.

THAT'S NOT TRUE! I'M BEING... **NORMAL** WITH YOU!

YOU'VE BEEN TREATING ME WEIRD EVER SINCE WE KISSED.

I THOUGHT YOU AND I WERE...

...FRIENDS AGAIN?

WE ARE **FRIENDS.** IT'S JUST WITH WHITNEY GONE, I'M AFRAID TO HANG OUT WITH YOU, BECAUSE...

I LIKE HER, JAKE. LIKE...**REALLY** LIKE HER.

I KNOW.

SO, I CAN'T STILL LIKE **YOU** IF I LIKE HER. BECAUSE MY LIKES ARE ALL RESERVED FOR HER. I HAVE NO LIKES LEFT.

I HAVE **FRIEND** LIKES BUT NOT **LIKE** LIKES...

SOPHIA? IT'S WONDERFUL TO MEET YOU, SWEETHEART.

SHE NEEDS A READING, WE NEED TO FIND A FRIEND OF HERS WHO'S A GHOST.

IS THAT SO?

TWENTY MINUTES LATER...

I'M SORRY TO DRAG YOU OVER HERE, BUT I FIGURED IT WAS A GOOD TIME TO TEACH CHARLOTTE ABOUT THE RULES HERE IN SPECTREVILLE.

MOM, THIS IS SO EMBARRASSING!

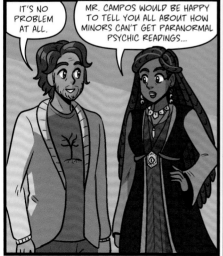

IT'S NO PROBLEM AT ALL.

MR. CAMPOS WOULD BE HAPPY TO TELL YOU ALL ABOUT HOW MINORS CAN'T GET PARANORMAL PSYCHIC READINGS...

...WITHOUT WRITTEN CONSENT FROM A PARENT OR GUARDIAN.

WAIT, DAD... YOU KNOW CHARLOTTE'S MOM?

ALRIGHT, MY DARLING...

...IT'S BEEN TOO LONG SINCE WE TALKED.

TALKED ABOUT WHAT?

YOU USED TO CONFIDE IN ME...

...BUT NOW I FIND OUT YOU'RE USING MS. RICHMOND TO SEARCH FOR YOUR GHOST FRIEND INSTEAD OF SHARING WITH ME--

BECAUSE WHITNEY'S STILL OUT THERE, BUT EVEN THOUGH YOU **KNOW** THAT, YOU'RE NOT HELPING ME FIND HER!

HOW DO YOU KNOW THAT?

FELIX OVERHEARD YOU AND MOM TALKING ABOUT IT. YOU HAD A SÉANCE AND GOT A MESSAGE FROM WHITNEY, BUT YOU **KEPT** IT FROM ME!

THAT'S WHY I CAN'T CONFIDE IN YOU... BECAUSE YOU **LIED** TO ME, DAD!

WHEEEEEEE

AND IT'S MORE THAN THAT. I USED TO FEEL SO CLOSE TO YOU, LIKE WE WERE A TEAM.

WHILE FELIX AND MOM WERE INTO SCIENCE AND GADGETS, YOU AND I USED **MAGIC**.

BUT INSTEAD OF BEING ON MY TEAM, YOU'RE PUSHING ME AWAY, FORCING ME OVER TO **THEIR** SIDE TO LEARN THINGS **THEIR** WAY AND--

ALRIGHT, THAT'S ENOUGH, MIJA.

WHY ARE YOU MAKING ME TAKE LESSONS FROM MOM AND NOT YOU?

÷SIGH.÷ WHEN FELIX TOOK MY SUPPLIES AND CAST THE BANISHMENT SPELL ON YOUR GHOST FRIEND, IT MADE YOUR MOTHER THINK THAT ME **AND** MY WAYS WERE... DANGEROUS.

I NEED TO PROVE TO HER THAT'S NOT THE CASE.

SO TEACH ME HOW TO USE MAGIC CORRECTLY, AND IT WON'T BE!

T'S MORE THAN THAT. R MOTHER'S METHODS E BASED IN LOGIC AND REASONING, SO THEY CARRY LESS RISK.

"SHE DOESN'T HAVE TO WORRY ABOUT THEM BACKFIRING AND CREATING A DANGEROUS SITUATION."

Field Notes

HEY, MOM, WHAT'S FOR DINNER?

OH! JUST GIVE ME... FIVE MINUTES TO CLEAN UP HERE.

"THAT'S WHY SHE HAS THE BUSINESS. FOR THE SAFETY OF THIS FAMILY."

COOL, WHATCHA WORKIN' ON?

JUST SOME STUFF FOR AN OLD PROJECT, DEFINITELY NOT MORE EXCITING THAN DINNER!

I NEED TO SHOW TO YOUR MOTHER I SUPPORT HER METHODS OVER MINE, RIGHT NOW.

YOU'RE TOO YOUNG TO UNDERSTAND, BUT IT'S--

IT'S THE ONLY WAY I CAN THINK OF TO GET HER BACK.

THE NEXT MORNING...

YOU AND I SHOULD START PRACTICING MAGIC TOGETHER.

STOP READING MY MIND.

THAT WAY WE CAN FIND WHITNEY AND I CAN PRACTICE THE CRAFT, AND WE CAN PROVE TO OUR PARENTS THAT WE'RE SMART AND MATURE ENOUGH TO START **DOING** THINGS.

GREAT. WHEN DO WE START?

LET'S MEET UP AFTER SCHOOL. HOW ABOUT THE CRYPTID CAFÉ, 3:00?

CRYPTID CAFÉ...

Dear Whitney,
I'm one step closer to getting you back.

I think you'd like my new friend Charlotte. She's confident and cool, and I feel like I fit in with her.

I guess she's a lot like you.

WHATCHA DOING?

FELIX! STOP LOOKING, THIS IS MY PRIVATE DIARY!

STILL PRETENDING YOU'RE PEN-PALS WITH A GHOST?

NONE OF YOUR BUSINESS. SHOULDN'T YOU BE AT LACROSSE OR SOMETHING?

NAH, NO PRACTICE TONIGHT. PLUS WE GOT THAT LESSON WITH MOM LATER.

HEY, I WANTED TO TALK TO YOU ABOUT THAT THOUGH-- REMEMBER LAST WEEK WHEN MOM WAS TELLING US ABOUT **POLTERGEISTS?**

...KIND OF.

≑PSH≑, I **KNEW** YOU WEREN'T PAYING ATTENTION.

ANYWAY, SHE SAID THAT THEY WORK ALONE -- LIKE IF THERE'S ONE POLTERGEIST IN YOUR HOUSE, THERE WON'T BE ANY MORE. THEY'RE TERRITORIAL, LIKE WOLVES. ONE WITHIN A CERTAIN RADIUS GUARANTEES THERE'S **ONLY** THE ONE.

SO WHAT?

WHAT ABOUT THOSE...DREAMS WE'VE ALL BEEN HAVING? WITH THE TWO-HEADED MONSTER? WHAT IF THAT THING REALLY IS **TWO** POLTERGEISTS? AND THAT'S WHY THEY'RE SO SCARY.

THOSE ARE JUST DREAMS, FELIX. REMEMBER, MOM AND DAD SAID THEY'RE JUST LIKE ECHOES, AFTER-EFFECTS OF THAT SPELL YOU CAST. THEY CAN'T HURT US.

BUT I CAN **FEEL** IT SOMETIMES, TOO. LIKE HEADACHES AND STUFF. THEY'RE NOT JUST DREAMS. MOM IS WORRIED TOO.

WHY DO YOU SAY THAT?

I SAW HER BUILDING SOMETHING THE OTHER DAY THAT SHE TRIED TO HIDE FROM ME.

I THINK IT'S SOMETHING TO USE **AGAINST** POLTERGEISTS. AND MAYBE IF I CAN FEEL WHEN IT'S NEARBY, I CAN --

HEY, GUYS!

OH, SORRY, DIDN'T MEAN TO SCARE YOU. HEY, SOPHIA'S LITTLE BROTHER, HOW ARE YOU? HERE TO JOIN OUR WITCHCRAFT PARTY?

⸲SIGH.⸲ WE'RE GOING TO STUDY UP ON SOME MAGIC STUFF TO TRY TO FIND WHITNEY. DON'T TELL MOM AND DAD, OKAY?

I WON'T! BUT SINCE YOU'RE DOING THAT...

WHAT IF I TRY TO SEE IF I CAN GET MOM'S TOOL TO WORK? IN CASE WE NEED THAT?

THAT SOUNDS LIKE **SKY FOX AND FESTER RAT** ARE TEAMING BACK UP!

I AM NOT FESTER RAT! I BETTER GET GOING...I'LL SEE YOU AT MOM'S TONIGHT, SIS.

YOU GUYS ARE SO CUTE, A LITTLE GHOST BUSTING INVESTIGATION TEAM. WHAT HAVE YOU GOT THERE?

OH...I'VE BEEN KEEPING TRACK OF THINGS SINCE WHITNEY'S BEEN GONE.

SO WHEN SHE GETS BACK, SHE DOESN'T FEEL LIKE SHE MISSED OUT. IT'LL BE LIKE SHE NEVER LEFT.

AW, WOW, THAT'S SO SWEET.

OH! **NOW** I GET IT. WHITNEY, THE GHOST GIRL... SHE'S YOUR **GIRLFRIEND!**

SHE'S NOT MY-- I MEAN--

I NEVER THOUGHT OF IT THAT WAY. I GUESS SHE...IS?

WICKED.

SO I SWIPED THIS BOOK FROM MY MOM'S PRIVATE STASH.

AAAAND I TOOK THIS FROM MY DAD'S, HAHA!

Practical Magic for MYSTICAL MINDED

SO I HEARD THAT THERE'S THIS HOLIDAY COMING UP CALLED **BELTANE**...

...WHERE THE VEIL BETWEEN THE LIVING AND THE DEAD IS THINNEST...

LATER THAT EVENING...

CRYPTID CAFÉ

I THINK WE'VE GOT ENOUGH INFO HERE TO START FORMING A WHITNEY PLAN, WHAT DO YOU THINK?

YEAH, I REALLY THINK BELTANE IS OUR TICKET.

NOW WE JUST NEED TO FIGURE OUT HOW FELIX'S TOOL CAN HELP.

MAN, WHO KNEW THERE WAS SO MUCH STUDYING--WHEN DO YOU GET TO THE ACTUAL **SPELL** CASTING?

SO WHEN WE LOOK FOR WHITNEY, WE'LL FIND HER THREE TIMES SOONER?

I CAN'T WAIT UNTIL I CAN SEE WHITNEY AGAIN...

I GUESS IT'S TRICKY ENOUGH THEY DON'T WANT YOU TO JUST JUMP INTO IT.

"ANY SPELL YOU CAST, GOOD OR BAD, WILL BE REVISITED ON YOU THREEFOLD".

I WAS GOING TO POINT OUT THAT YOUR BOYFRIEND JUST WALKED IN, BUT NOW THAT I KNOW YOU'RE IN LOVE WITH WHITNEY...

...YOU WOULDN'T MIND IF I ASKED HIM OUT, WOULD YOU?

WHAT? YOU...YOU LIKE JAKE?

I THINK HE'S REALLY CUTE, YEAH. AND YOU SAID HE'S A FRIEND OF YOURS AND SUPER NICE, RIGHT?

I THOUGHT THIS WAS ABOUT YOU PROVING YOUR SKILL AT CONTROLLING POLTERGEISTS WITH YOUR TOOLS, NOT ABOUT EARL.

I THOUGHT IF I COULD GET EARL BACK, IT WOULD PROVE THAT I'M NOT A MURDERER...

OH, SWEETHEART.

I JUST NEED TO FIX THIS.

EWWWW!

WHAT ARE YOU TWO... **DOING?**

FELIX, SHUSH!

IT'S NONE OF YOUR BUSINESS WHAT WE WERE DOING.

ALRIGHT, MY CHILDREN, BE GOOD TO YOUR MOTHER-- SOPHIA, I'LL BE BACK TO GET YOU IN TWO HOURS!

ENOUGH DILLY-DALLYING, KIDS, LET'S GET STARTED.

I'M NOT SURE ANYMORE... WE'RE IN A MAZE BUT WE'RE NOT ALONE...THERE'S A TWO-HEADED MONSTER THAT'S BEEN CHASING US. WE SAW A PORTAL OPEN UP THAT LOOKED LIKE IT LED SOMEWHERE OUT, BUT I THINK IT NEEDS TO BE MORE **POWERFUL** TO WORK--

WE HAVE TO MOVE AGAIN! THIS PLACE IS SO WEIRD, I'M STARTING TO FORGET THINGS! TELL SOPHIA--

WHITNEY?!

ALRIGHT YOUNG LADY, THAT IS **IT**... YOU ARE OFFICIALLY GROUNDED.

I'M SORRY, MOM, I KNOW I'M NOT SUPPOSED TO PLAY AROUND WITH MAGIC YET...

...BUT THERE'S SOMETHING I NEED TO TELL SOPHIA--

GROUND-ED.

Knock Knock

JAKE! HI--

CHARLOTTE WANTS YOU TO MEET HER AT THE MYSTERY SPOT AT 8:00PM TONIGHT. FOR SOMETHING CALLED "BELTANE."

YOU SAW CHARLOTTE?

SHE SAID SHE WAS GROUNDED, OTHERWISE SHE'D BE TELLING YOU HERSELF. LATER.

JAKE! THANK YOU FOR PASSING THAT ALONG TO ME, I APPRECIATE IT!

I TOLD YOU BEFORE I WANTED TO HELP, SO I DON'T SEE WHY YOU'RE SURPRISED THAT I **CAN** ACTUALLY HELP--

...YOU'RE RIGHT, I'M SORRY. AND IF CHARLOTTE'S GROUNDED, SHE'S GOING TO NEED YOUR HELP TOO. I'LL TELL YOU EVERYTHING WE'RE PLANNING FOR THE MYSTERY SPOT TONIGHT...

...BUT FIRST WE NEED TO CALL FELIX.

I KNOW, RIGHT? I FOUND HER! SHE WAS ONLY THERE FOR A SECOND, BUT SHE SAID WE NEEDED TO COME SOMEPLACE MORE POWERFUL TO GET HER OUT. AND THEN I REMEMBERED YOUR TOUR...I FIGURED WHAT PLACE IS MORE POWERFUL THAN THE ONE THAT **PULLED** SETTLERS HERE IN THE FIRST PLACE?

DID SHE SAY ANYTHING ELSE? ABOUT WHERE SHE WAS? OR HOW SHE WAS DOING?

UNFORTUNATELY, NO. THAT'S WHEN MY MOM INTERRUPTED AND GROUNDED ME FOR UNDERAGE MAGICKING.

YEAH, I CAN'T IMAGINE MY MOM REACTING WELL IF SHE CAUGHT ME DOING MAGIC, EITHER.

THAT WAS REALLY BRAVE OF YOU, CHARLOTTE.

LUCKILY MINE COULD PROBABLY CARE LESS.

HAHA, GOOD, SO IF WE GET CAUGHT, WE'LL JUST BOTH HIDE BEHIND JAKE! SO WHAT'S YOUR SPELL?

WELL...IT SAID IT WAS KIND OF ADVANCED, BUT WE BOTH COME FROM STRONG LINES OF WITCHES, RIGHT?

HEH. OR WE **HOPE** WE DO, ANYWAY!

IT'S CALLED "HANDFASTING." IF WE CAN FIND WHITNEY, WE CAN USE IT TO BIND ME TO HER...AND DRAG HER OUT OF WHEREVER SHE IS.

FELIX, WHAT'S HAPPENING?

TAKE **THAT, YOU** STUPID POLTERGEIST! I SHOWED YOU WHAT YOU CAN DO WITH YOUR DUMB NIGHTMARES AND HEADACHES, DIDN'T I?

I SEE HER! I CAN SEE WHITNEY NOW!

WHITNEY?

VWOOOOO~

GRUMM

WAP

IT... IT REALLY WORKED...

WHITNEY, IT LOOKED LIKE SOMETHING... OR SOMEONE...WAS COMING OUT OF THE PIT BEFORE YOU. WERE YOU ALONE DOWN THERE?

THERE WAS SOMEONE ELSE?! I DIDN'T SEE ANYONE BUT THE MONSTER...

MAYBE IT WAS A TRICK OF THE LIGHT? LIKE, WHO ELSE COULD BE DOWN THERE?

I...I CAN'T REMEMBER... ANYTHING...

...WHITNEY...DO YOU REMEMBER **US?**

...YES. YES, I REMEMBER. YOU'RE MY SOPHIA.

charmz chat

Monica Gallagher is the writer and co-creator of GFFs. She has over ten years experience making comics and illustrations with a positive feminist spin. She has worked for Oni Press, Vertigo, and Valiant, as well as self-published several of her own comics at her website, eatyour-lipstick.com. Her latest webcomic is Assassin Roommate, updated weekly on Webtoons.

Kata Kane is the artist and co-creator of GFFs. She is also the artist on ANA AND THE COSMIC RACE from Charmz, the creator of Altar Girl, and she loves to draw comics for all ages and young adults. She loves watching anime and reading manga such as Sailor Moon. You can find more of her comicbooks and artwork at kata-kane.com.

We asked our Charmz creators a few questions about GFFs and present their answers here...

How did the two of you come up with the idea for GFFs?

Kata Kane: Monica had the really cool story idea of a spooky old tourist town where ghosts and spirits were the norm, so that was how we founded the town of Spectreville. I added some character ideas for a family that could be investigators in the town: a sister

and brother duo who didn't always get along and had very different methods of how to deal with their work. We knew we needed a ghost character that could be Sophia's first solo job... but Whitney was much more and we knew from the beginning she would become the love interest for Sophia!

Monica Gallagher: Spectreville is a

Charlotte

Rebecca

Earl

Monica Gallagher: I find all the scientific tools really fun and fascinating, but since ghosts and the paranormal aren't logical and clear cut, it makes sense to me that the methods of investigating them wouldn't be either! Overall I think it has to be a blended approach, but I also get really into the fun of the more out there mystical techniques.

Do you have any advice for those who want to create their own comics?

shout-out to my love of the ghost tours that have been springing up in small towns throughout this country. I've always wanted to do a story involving ghost characters, so I thought it'd be a nice change to put them in a place that had already accepted (and was enthusiastic about!) ghosts and the paranormal in general. I was also interested in ideas involving romance when it involved not gender, but the person you fall in love with. And Kata was a terrific collaborator with bouncing ideas off of and fleshing out all the characters.

Kata Kane: Start writing and drawing now! Even if you think it won't be perfect. It's okay to make mistakes and to learn from them. The more you practice creating comics for yourself, the better you'll get. Sometimes I just start with a character idea, and the story gets built around them. You should always create something that makes you happy!

Monica Gallagher: Definitely just keep doing it! Don't be afraid to put stuff out there, and to keep putting stuff out there. Plus it's really important to finish something, not put off doing something because what you have in mind is a giant story. None of us who create are ever 100% satisfied and happy with what we put out there, but the fun of it is seeing what you come up with and watching your own style grow and improve!

If you were a Paranormal Investigator like Sophia and Felix's family, would you use "scientific tools" or "magical witchcraft"?

Kata Kane: I think it is all pretty magical in Spectreville to be able to see ghosts, but I would probably try to use research like Felix and his mom Joanne do to figure out the best methods for dealing with the spirits. I really like that Sophia and her dad Oscar are good at communicating with ghosts and understanding what the ghosts need emotionally too.

Thanks Monica and Kata! If you have a question for either Monica or Kata or both, send it to us at salicrup@papercutz.com.

And now a special sneak peek at AMY'S DIARY #1 "Space Alien…Almost?"

SEPTEMBER
The End of the World

-Tuesday, September 13th-

7:05pm:
Sometimes I feel alone in the universe. I don't get along with anybody, except for my best friend, Kat, but ever since we got into an argument over something stupid, we're not talking anymore. There's my mom, of course, (she's downstairs in the kitchen making some spaghetti sauce and it smells soooooo good), but I can't really tell her everything and she gets on my nerves sometimes. Like right now.

7:10pm: My mom's calling me to tell me dinner's ready.

7:12pm: Okay, I'll go downstairs and eat…But first, I've got to point out that I'm being punished, because I made a little, let's say, "behavior mistake" at school. Honestly, I don't deserve my punishment. I just played a little joke on the math teacher (who, let me point out, has been a real pain since the beginning of the year). She shouted in class: "You must follow the process or you'll miss the train for your diploma!" And I answered: "We'll catch a boat…" and then found myself in the principal's office:

Dennis Belcher…

7:16pm: Okay, I've got to go have dinner.

8:35pm: Great…My mom's decided my punishment would be not getting to watch "One Tree Hill." That sucks! What's more, she told me the principal wanted to see her tomorrow to talk about my grades. Tssk! I was just starting to hate him when she said: "He's cute."

Cute handsome? Or cute nice? Argh!

Does she have a crush on him or something?!

10:00pm: My mom came into to my room and saw me crying. She told me she didn't know "One Tree Hill" was that important to me and let me watch it on my computer. But I wasn't crying about that. I was crying because I was thinking about my dad, who's not here anymore…

I feel like telling her the Britney Spears thing is totally stupid.

It's true, though, I just screwed up.

It popped out of my mouth all by itself because I was so proud of her performance on the Dance Dance Revolution!

It's not like I blabbed she had pimples all over her body! She doesn't, anyhow...

Maybe I should show her the answers for my test in "Miss Magazine," which say we're supposed to be friends for life.

Miss Magazine Test

friends 4-ever

Are You Girl Friends For Life?

Being friends isn't always easy!
But we deepen our ties by getting past obstacles.
Take the test to find out if your friendship is made to last!

Best friend ♡

1: One of you tells THE OTHER a secret. What happens?

A ARCHEOLOGISTS WILL BE NEEDED TO REVEAL THIS SECRET IN A MILLION YEARS! ☒

B YOU CAN TRUST HER, BUT YOU DON'T TELL HER ANYTHING, JUST IN CASE.

C THE WHOLE SCHOOL WILL KNOW ABOUT IT BY THE NEXT DAY. ☐

2. YOUR GIRL FRIEND THINKS YOUR BOYFRIEND IS SO GORGEOUS

A DANGER! DANGER! MY FRIEND MIGHT BECOME A RIVAL. ☐

B MY BEST FRIEND WOULD NEVER GO OUT WITH MY BOYFRIEND

C WELL, MY OUTINGS WITH MY BOYFRIEND WILL BE WITHOUT HER.

Don't miss AMY'S DIARY #1 coming Winter 2019!

Can Crimson stop the ghost hamsters? Find out in STITCHED #2, on sale now wherever books are sold!

SMOKEY MOUNTAIN: TONDO, MANILA. THE PHILIPPINES.

BEAUTY QUEEN is coming soon wherever books are sold from

THANK YOU VERY MUCH, FRIENDS!

RENATA! COME HERE, IHA!

I HAVE TO GO. SEE YOU LATER!

RENATA, GO BUY SOME RICE AND DRIED FISH WITH WHAT YOUR KUYA GETS FOR THE PICKINGS. BRING *PONSO* WITH YOU.

YES, *NANAY.*